ALASTAIR REID

I Will Tell You of a Town

Illustrated by W. Lorraine

1 9 5 6

HOUGHTON MIFFLIN COMPANY BOSTON

The Riverside Press, Cambridge

LISTEN. AND WATCH. If you perch up here with the sea-gulls, high on the cliff, I will tell you of a town. It is early, early morning, and the sun is growing big and round like a bright orange over the sea. The sky is turning to blue and gold, and the sea is blue and gold to match it. The waves and the clouds are dancing, and the dark·is blowing away over the edge of the world. Now, if you look down under your feet, you will see cuddling close to the cliff for shelter a little town, silent and asleep, curled up in its own dream.

Do you know what a town really is? It is not one thing, but a mystifying mixture of houses and streets, cats and birds, people and windows and bells and clocks and schools and smells, all jumbled together on a little piece of the earth, a place for children and grandfathers, a place for growing up and growing old. There would be no people without houses, and no houses without people, so nobody can say how it began.

Do you see down there where, past the square and the tall clock tower with its polished face, past the store full of fishnets, past the statues and the school, wanders one lazy street called Halibut Street, looking

2

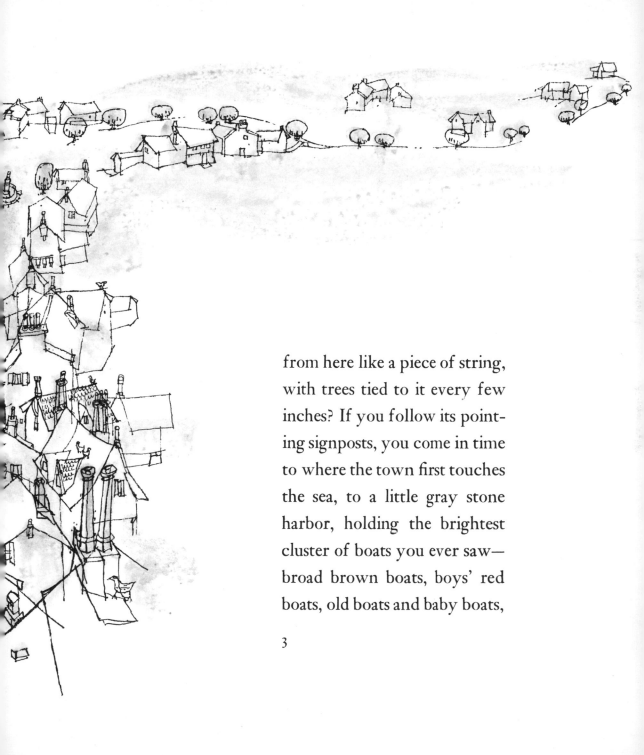

from here like a piece of string, with trees tied to it every few inches? If you follow its point-ing signposts, you come in time to where the town first touches the sea, to a little gray stone harbor, holding the brightest cluster of boats you ever saw— broad brown boats, boys' red boats, old boats and baby boats,

3

sad boats, bent boats, shiny boats, and dead boats, boats in ones
and twos, with masts and wires and nets and lamps and cabins
and flags, stirring slowly in the water, and all waiting. Waiting,
because this is a fishing town, and every day, from dawn till
dark, the boats go out on an endless search for fish.

Listen now. The old clock in the tower is stirring itself.
Hear it take a deep breath, whirring its wheels and weights.
Suddenly, with a sound like a stroke of luck, *BONG* goes
the first loud brass bell of the day. *BONG, BONG, BONG,*

BONG and the sound of the bell swells and bursts and runs over the red roofs, down chimneys, in windows, under doors,

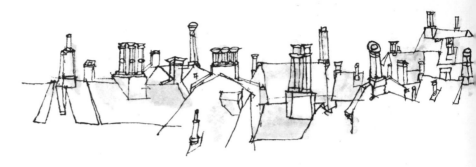

through keyholes, into the drowsy puffed pillows in the dozing houses. One by one heads lift, eyes open, hands clasp

covers, and children wink awake and lie listening to the golden bell telling them it is morning.

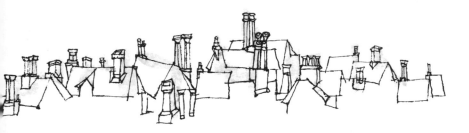

All over town sleepers stretch themselves, pull on clothes, and look out to wonder about the weather. From the high

attics fishermen crinkle their eyes, asking questions of the clouds, noticing the surface of the sea crumpled like knitting, and the sun climbing steadily up the sheet of the sky. A fine day for fishing, say the clouds. Come and dance with

us, call the waves. Breakfast is busy cooking itself in the
kitchen, and soon, as "Goodbye, goodbye" sounds every-
where, out of all the opening doors, red doors, green doors,
doors with brass knobs, doors with glass eyes, doors with
knockers and bells, and doors which just squeak, come clump-
ing the fishermen in their big rubber boots, into Halibut
Street, through the square, laughing, calling, lighting big
pipes, rubbing sleepy eyes, down the hill on their way to the
harbor, waving cheerful farewells to the faces they have left
behind in the windows.

8

Now what is going to happen? Follow the wheeling falling gulls as they dive and drift from their nests on the cliff, down, down, down on light wings to perch on a harbor lamp or a driftwood box, and watch again. Watch the broadbacked, big-shouldered fishermen calling good morning to the sea, and swinging down the clanging iron ladders to the decks of the boats below. Follow this one, with his face full of white whiskers, his pipe puffing a tune, and his eyes dancing in the morning sun. Old Daniel, he is called by the others. He takes longer on the ladder, for he has been sailing the years away since he was a boy, longer than anyone can remember. Behind him come his two sons, with brown nets slung on their shoulders, whistling in the clean air, and hoping for fish.

Old Daniel's boat, *The Whisk*, is built for the rolling sea, stout and steady and red and neat as an apple, from its shining brass binnacle to its fluttering flag at the bow. Amidships, a hatch is open over the empty hold, the big square space which has to be filled with fish. The boys climb below to the cabin, dumping their duffle bags on the small bunks, pulling on their sea boots, coiling lines, oiling the engine, checking the gear for the long sail out. The nets are piled tidily round the edge of the deck. Everything is ready, and Old Daniel, behind the wheel, whistles to the boys to slip the lines as the motor splutters and sings, and *The Whisk* rocks on the tide.

All over the harbor, orders are shouted, nets are folded, knots are loosened, and engines snort. The wind brings a mixture of smoke and laughter as it twitches the flags and ropes and Old Daniel's white whiskers. Smell the oil and the tar. Watch the scrubbed decks swinging and the masts swaying, and feel the air full of the excitement of sailing. In a minute—now, *The Whisk* slips from its mooring, very slowly, and edges toward the mouth of the harbor, as though it were feeling with its nose the coldness of the sea outside. One by one the boats crawl away from their lines, with the men waving and shouting, and the gulls rising in a cloud of wings, croaking their sad goodbyes, and blowing back over the harbor. Shade your eyes as the boats turn together into the path of the sun, across the speckled water and away. And listen. As if at a signal, the little flags fly up to the mastheads, and over the water comes the sound of whistles, blowing goodbye from the bobbing boats to the town left behind.

And can you see what the town is doing? From windows

and doorways and gardens and roofs, a hundred handker-
chiefs and tablecloths and scarves are being flown like kites
full of farewells. The town buzzes with goodbyes. The bell
rumbles in the clock tower, the children squeak from the
highest rooms, mothers wave aprons and cats wave their tails,
until the boats are black dots, almost lost on the wide blue
counterpane of the sea. Then quietly the town, emptied of
deep voices, settles down to its waiting day.

THE DAY IS TICKING AWAY, and the old clock, which has watched over the town for centuries, is counting the children on their shouting way to school. Six little fishing children from the corner cottage, five from the red house by the fire station, four from the farm, three from the white lighthouse, twins from the gardener's hut, and one alone, little Billy from the bakery, waving to his mother with a red woolen cap. They meet in the playground, and mix and chatter and push till schooltime, watched by old Archer, the school cat, who nibbles his tongue and nods good day. Every day, Archer

15

waits sleepily for
the school door to close
and the books to open, and
then he stretches himself like elastic,
and saunters to the center of the square.

Come down and walk on the cobbles now, and see what he is after. Look. Up Halibut Street from the harbor, lumbering on squeaky wheels, comes a lurching cart, heaped up high with fish. It seems to be moving by itself, but suddenly over the top of it pops a head, and a voice like a baby trumpet calls *FISH* into the air till windows pop open, and the chimney smoke ties itself in knots. "Fish," whispers the echo all over

waits sleepily for
the school door to close
and the books to open, and
then he stretches himself like elastic,
and saunters to the center of the square.

Come down and walk on the cobbles now, and see what he is after. Look. Up Halibut Street from the harbor, lumbering on squeaky wheels, comes a lurching cart, heaped up high with fish. It seems to be moving by itself, but suddenly over the top of it pops a head, and a voice like a baby trumpet calls *FISH* into the air till windows pop open, and the chimney smoke ties itself in knots. "Fish," whispers the echo all over

THE DAY IS TICKING AWAY, and the old clock, which has watched over the town for centuries, is counting the children on their shouting way to school. Six little fishing children from the corner cottage, five from the red house by the fire station, four from the farm, three from the white lighthouse, twins from the gardener's hut, and one alone, little Billy from the bakery, waving to his mother with a red woolen cap. They meet in the playground, and mix and chatter and push till schooltime, watched by old Archer, the school cat, who nibbles his tongue and nods good day. Every day, Archer

15

And where have you gone? Oh, I see you there, perched on the steeple with your gull-friends. And what are you watching? The houses, the houses, a townful of houses. They are perched on one another's shoulders, houses with white-washed walls and red roofs, watching with their window eyes, and listening with their chimneys for a sound from the sea. Peer down through the skylights into the dusty attics cluttered with sea chests and lanterns. In winter, when the town is muffled with woolen snow, the lanterns wink their green eyes out of the high attics, and the sailors, seeing them from their cold boats at sea, think then of warm things, friends and families, a safe supper, slippers, and a soft bed.

But underneath the attics? Fly high over the town to one crooked weatherbeaten house above the harbor, slip down the skylight and the laddery stairs, hide, and look slowly around you. Fishermen spend so much time at sea that they make their boats like homes and their homes like boats, as if they could never decide which is which. All round the room there are odds and ends from the sea—a brass bell by the door, ships' lamps swinging from the ceiling, bunks to sleep in, and in one corner, a tiny ship's hammock with a

The housewives hurry back
and forward from his barrow, smiling,
and carrying big woven baskets. Mungo
winks at the clock in the tower, and the clock
ticks back. The barrow grows lighter and lighter,
till the last coin tinkles in Mungo's pocket. Fishtime is
over, Archer is asleep, and Mungo goes limping back to
chat with the town's twelve grandfathers on the sea wall.

19

Fish for the family, fresh fish, fat fish,
codfish, crayfish, dogfish, catfish,
whiskery fish with fans for tails,
big fish, baby fish, fish for frying,
sighing fish with silvery scales.

I will tell you a swimming story,
under the sea and nine bells down.
Fishbones, funnybones, hung on a fishhook,
goggling fish for a capable fishcook,
haddock and mackerel,
herring and whiting,
fish for the whole wide town.

the little cobbled alleys. "Mungo the Fishman is calling 'Fish!'"
Archer the cat grins from whisker to whisker as round the
cluttered fishcart Mungo comes limping on a wooden leg to
throw him a quicksilver fish. Mungo is red and fat and full
of stories and news of the weather and the world. Bump,
bump, goes his wooden leg, and as he sells the shining fish he
sings the same song always to the town.

baby singing in it. By the fire an old man is sitting on a ship's
stool, busy with his fingers. Come very close now to watch
him, and hold your breath. Inside a bulging green bottle, on
a small sea of its own, he has slipped a miniature ship, so small
that your fingers look like whales beside it. It has puffed
cotton-wool sails, paper flags, matchbox hatches, and an
anchor like a pin. How did it get inside? If you ask the old
man, he will only wink at you, and say it is a secret, as it is
when you hear the sound of the sea in a shell. And round the
room, you will see bottles of all shapes and sizes, each with

a small shrunken ship inside, until you feel you are under
water, and would not be surprised if you looked out of the
round porthole windows and saw fish goggling in at you.

But what is that buzzing? Quick, quick, back to the square;
for school is coming out, like an explosion. Out into the sun
pours a whole schoolful of children, let loose from books
and blackboards, names and numbers, singing and spelling.
They are turning cartwheels and shouting all over the caper-
ing square. Come closer now, and hear what they are saying
into the air. Listen.

Why is China pink? The map says so.

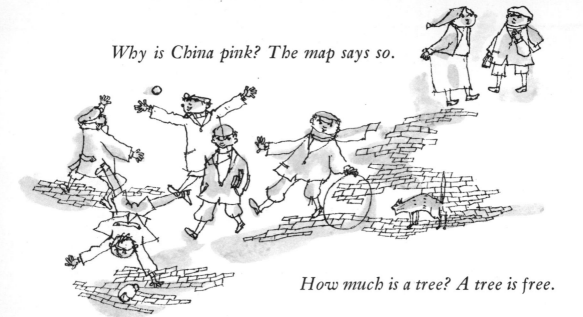

How much is a tree? A tree is free.

What is the time? Anytime. Ten minutes past tea.

Where is Mungo? Mungo is listening.

Listening to what? Listening to the cockleshells.

What do the shells say? The shells say the sea.

Why doesn't the sea run away, like my bath?

When is Friday? Ten tides away.

Old Daniel said he'd put me in a bottle for being bad.

My father caught fifty flounders last Friday.

Fifty? Well, forty. Forty? Well, five.

When do the boats come? Anytime now, when the tide tells them.

25

The words whirl up like butterflies over the lighthouse. But hurry. It is time to get back to the clock over the square, counting, counting. There is always something to count in the town—children in their games, nets hung up to dry, new flowers open in the gardens, gulls sitting on their nests, grandmothers knitting in the shade. Counting chimneys and children, flowers and fishnets, boats and babies, the old clock's day is full, and the time is past before it is noticed. And, after all, what is time but all the things that happen, head over heels, in a day's business?

Already the sun is falling, and everyone is looking up at the clock. It is higher here than anywhere else in the town, and you can see far, far out to sea. The water looks smooth as a tablecloth—but what is that speck on the blue distance, almost too far away to tell? A seabird perhaps, or a floating box? No, it grows bigger, and there are others. The boats! The crooked whistle on the lighthouse starts to squeal, and the sound runs wild as wind, telling the town. Doors squeak open and crash shut. Feet patter on the cobbles, children's chattering feet, the hasty feet of the fishermen's wives, old feet, cold feet, the hobbling boots of the grandfathers,

Mungo's bumping pegleg, and the soft bare feet of the run-
away boys, all hurrying to the sea wall. Shawls wave in the
wind, the lines are ready, the clock begins to count faster,
and the empty barrels wait for fish. The whole town quivers
with little bubbles of excitement; for the boats are coming
home.

Now, YOU MUST FLY as high as you can, and look down; and you will see the town lying below you like a map, the sea deep blue, the land green, and the streets spread out like a spiderweb, with people like insects scurrying to the harbor. The boats look like toys in a blue bath, creeping in twos and threes toward the shore, leaving long white disappearing lines behind them in the water. You may catch the flash of silver

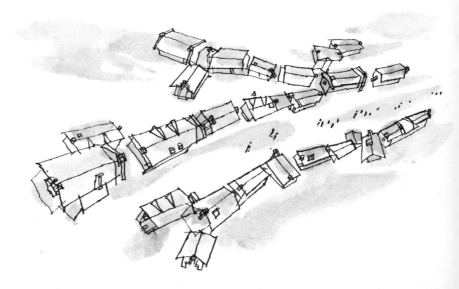

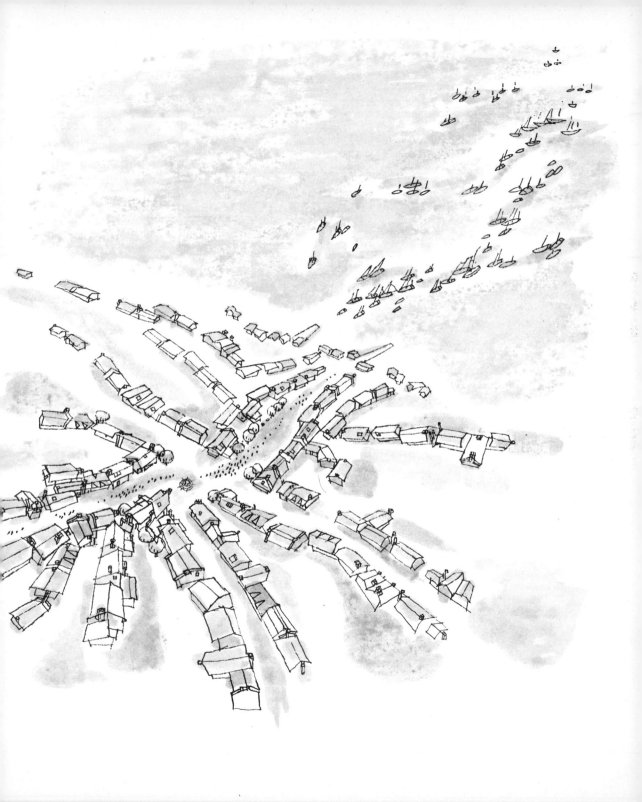

in the holds, for those spaces that were hollow in the morning are now overflowing with tumbling silver fish. Gulls swoop and hope for a spare herring, and in the clear evening air you can hear their calls mixing with the hum of the motors, and the men shouting as they turn their boats in a wide circle into the waiting harbor.

Now everything happens so swiftly that you hardly know where to watch. Everyone in the whole town seems to be here, all busy except the twelve grandfathers, who shout advice to the others. The fishermen, singing and sunburned, are heaving away at netfuls of fish. The children bring bas-

kets, or roll fat barrels in rows. Hands, arms, and voices all work at top speed, so that the sea-wall buzzes with life. For once, the old clock is breathless. It cannot count, because everybody is going too fast. So it gives up ticking and listens instead to the hubbub of voices blowing up Halibut Street.

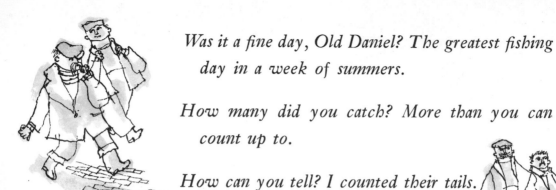

Was it a fine day, Old Daniel? The greatest fishing day in a week of summers.

How many did you catch? More than you can count up to.

How can you tell? I counted their tails.

What's for supper? Wait and see.

Race you round the harbor. Three times round.

I found a fish that spoke to me. What did it say?

It said Old Daniel's boat was the best on the sea.

Mother, how many? Forty full barrels and one
over for Mungo.

Will it rain tonight? The clouds say no but my
bones say yes.

Will the fish get wet? No, fish are waterproof.

Today is wind day and tomorrow is wash day.
Home, home, all go home.

And home they go, as the blue in the air gets deeper and deeper and darker and darker, and the water swishes slowly against the stones and grows black. The lanterns wink on and the light breaks into big golden pennies on the sea. Everyone winds up Halibut Street, calling goodnight to the birds and the boats, home to a steaming supper in the shiny kitchens, home to talk about the day and to tell their stories. But listen. Out of the houses comes the sound of singing, deep voices, gruff voices, girls' voices, children's voices like little bells. Even a cat's mewing voice joins in the chorus. And for the joy of a good day on the sea, they sing this song to the fish.

34

A fish lost his way in the looking-glass sea
and he swam himself silly till he swam to me;
then he nibbled at my net and slipped inside
and sighed "Can I sleep? I'm tired of the tide.

It's too much trouble
to goggle and bubble,
and swim all day
in a lazy way.
I don't want to drown.
I want to come to town.
I want to be dry,
but don't ask me why."

Some fish are silly and some fish are flat,
but who ever heard of a fish like that?

Now, below you, under a blanket of dark, the town is spread in its dream. The wind wanders there, breathing under doors, hushing the babies to sleep, carrying out to sea the smoke from chimneys and the whiff of fish, and clearing the clouds from the great silver moon, hung like a balloon in the sky. Archer the cat is curled up asleep in a fishnet. Somewhere a dog grumbles in the darkness, and a last sleepy grandfather turns his eyes to the horizon to watch the weather and the changing castles in the clouds; and then the lights blink out, one by one, in all the little windows.

Swish, swish. The waves are hushing on the beach. Sleep, sleep. The dogs are dreaming of bones. The boats in the harbor stir slowly round and bump softly together as the tide turns. The seagulls fold their careful wings, and the chickens cluck softly in the still farmyard. Only the light in the lighthouse is still awake, blinking a welcome or a warning to any ships at sea, across the rocks and the chasing tides.

The old clock, ticking the heartbeats of the town, is counting himself drowsy under the single, wishing moon. Now the sea and the sky talk together on the edge of the land, the language of water and clouds; and in the middle of those three great spaces, far below, is lying the town. There, laughter and tears change places like waves and tides. There, children grow old, and old men grow young again. There, always, you can watch a day rise and fall, a day like the one you have been watching, a day that is every day. Rest now. And soon enough, the sun will come up over the edge of the never-ending sea, the town will open its windows to the morning, and the day that has just ended will be ready to begin all over again.